D0594450

HOW LITTLE GREY RABBIT
GOT BACK HER TAIL

How Little Grey Rabbit Got Back Her Tail
first published in Great Britain in 1929 by William
Heinemann Limited

This edition first published in Great Britain in 1984 by

Octopus Books Limited
59 Grosvenor Street
London W1

ISBN 0 7064 2203 1

Produced by
Mandarin Publishers Limited
22a Westlands Road
Quarry Bay, Hong Kong

Printed in Hong Kong

HOW LITTLE GREY RABBIT
GOT BACK HER TAIL

BY ALISON UTTLEY

ILLUSTRATIONS BY MARGARET TEMPEST

OCTOPUS BOOKS LIMITED

One cold March morning Little Grey Rabbit awoke at dawn and lay for a moment looking round her dim white-washed attic. Then she jumped out of bed, washed her face and paws, and slipped on her grey dress with its white collar and cuffs. Round her waist she tied a blue apron, for this was to be a busy day.

Softly she opened her door and listened. Snores could be heard coming from Hare's room, and squeaky little grunts from Squirrel's. They were both fast asleep!

She crept downstairs like a shadow, and went into the kitchen. From a hook she took down a round wicker basket and then she went out into the raw air.

T he sun had not risen, and a star was still in the sky, 'like a candle for a little rabbit,' she thought.

As she walked down the garden path she looked back at the shut windows, and waved a paw to her sleeping friends in the little house.

She turned down the lane and scampered over the stones, leaping over thorny briars, and swinging her basket round and round over her head.

A startled Mouse scuttled into the hedge and gazed after her with astonished eyes. 'Grey Rabbit is off early this morning,' he told his wife. 'I wonder where she is going? It's a pity she's lost her tail, she must feel cold. They say it is fastened up on Wise Owl's door, but may I never see it!'

He curled his own tail round and settled down to sleep again.

The Rabbit came to an opening in a hedge, by a wildrose bush, now bare and spiney, and she climbed through, tearing her apron on a curved thorn.

She stopped to pin it with a straight pin from a hawthorn bush, and to sip the water from a gurgling spring, like a small fountain in the grass.

Then she ran across the wet meadow to a bank where the first primroses were growing, with petals closed, asleep on their green leaves in the early light.

She put down her basket and began to pick them, biting off their pink stalks, and putting the yellow blossoms in the basket.

Her little nose twitched with pleasure as she worked among the sweet smells, and she rubbed herself on the leaves to get the scent in her hair. When she finished there, she ran to another field, and another, and another, with a basket now heaped with petals. Behind her she left a trail of small footprints which scarcely pressed down the grey-green grass.

Suddenly a black nose and two pink hands with funny little human fingers stuck out of the earth in front of her. She started back.

'Oh! Oh! Moldy Warp, how you frightened me!' she exclaimed, with her paw on her fluttering heart. 'Wherever have you come from?'

'I was asleep, Grey Rabbit, but you woke me, pit-pattering just over my pillow, so I came out to see who it was,' and the Mole shook off the red soil clinging to his bare feet and wiped his hands on the grass.

'How are the Hare and Squirrel?' he asked politely, picking up the primroses Grey Rabbit had dropped in her fright.

'Squirrel is very well, but Hare has a bad cold. He sat in a draught last week, watching March come in like a Lion, and he has sneezed ever since.'

hat are you doing out here so early, Grey Rabbit?'

'I am picking primroses for Primrose Wine,' answered the Rabbit. 'It's a certain cure for a cold. My mother used to make it. These are the first primroses, so they are the sweetest, and they will make the best wine. Besides, I've picked them with the dew on them.'

'What a clever Rabbit you are!' said the Mole admiringly. 'But where is your tail?' he added, blinking his small eyes.

Grey Rabbit told how she gave her tail to Wise Owl in return for his advice on gardening.

'I didn't know Owl was a gardener,' said Moldy Warp shortly.

11

thought I was the best digger hereabouts,' and he proudly held up his hands and spread out his fingers.

'Of course you are, Moldy; there is no one like you except Badger. Owl advised me about seeds, carrot seed, lettuce seed, so that we could grow food ourselves.'

'Oh! He did, did he?' muttered the Mole; 'and he took your tail, did he?'

'No, I gave it to him,' returned Grey Rabbit sadly.

Mole and the Rabbit sat on the bank among the primrose leaves and watched the green sky with its baby pink cloudlets change as the great red sun lifted itself out of the bath of mist.

'Grey Rabbit,' said the Mole solemnly, 'would you like your tail back, very very much?'

'Very very much,' answered Grey Rabbit mournfully, 'but Owl is a kind of friend, and he must not be made my enemy.'

'I'll help you, Grey Rabbit,' said the Mole, striking his breast with his hand, just as a long level sunray shone across the field and turned his velvet waistcoat red. 'I will think out a plan and we will get it back.'

'Good-bye, and thank you, Moldy Warp,' said the Rabbit. 'I must run now, or I shall be late for breakfast,' and off she ran with her flowers bobbing up and down in the basket.

t the Little House by the Wood, there was dismay when Grey Rabbit was missed. Hare ran up and down-stairs with his head in a red cotton handkerchief, calling, 'Where are you, Grey Rabbit? A-tishoo! Are you hiding, Grey Rabbit? A-tishoo!'

But Squirrel saw the basket was gone, and guessed the Rabbit was busy somewhere.

'Help me to get the breakfast, Hare, instead of calling like that,' she scolded.

Hare wiped his eyes with a corner of the handkerchief, sneezed violently, and blew a bunch of camomile off the shelf. 'A-tishoo! A-tishoo!' went he, and the little brown teapot rocked on the table.

'Oh, do be careful!' exclaimed Squirrel. 'What will Grey Rabbit say if she finds the tea-pot on the floor?'

'Grey Rabbit thinks more of my cold than of the old tea-pot,' said Hare, as he swept the tablecloth off the table and wrapped it round his shoulders. 'She is sympa-what-do-you-call-it, and you are not.'

'No, I am not sympa-what-do-you-call-it,' said Squirrel, indignantly seizing the cloth and shaking it. She reset the table, and made a dish of scrambled ants' eggs. She minced a bunch of grass and flavoured it with carrot and turnip from the store-house. She filled the three plates, put them on the table, and drew up the chairs.

'R at-a-tat-tat,' came Hedgehog with the milk.

'Late again! Have you seen Grey Rabbit?' asked Squirrel. Hedgehog shook his old head. 'No,' said he, 'I've been too busy a-milking my cow. She wouldn't lie still this morning, and I had to chase her all over the field. At my time of life, too. Is Little Grey Rabbit missing?'

'Of course she is or I should not ask you,' snapped the Squirrel, who began to feel anxious.

'Sorry, no offence,' said the Hedgehog, picking up his milkcan and shuffling down the path.

'I can't abide that pair,' he muttered, 'though Robin says they are a deal better since Grey Rabbit rescued them from the Weasel.

'Now little Grey Rabbit is a nice little thing.'

A light footstep came up the lane and a voice was heard singing:

'Primroses, Primroses,
Primroses fine,
Pick them and press them
And make yellow wine.'

The Grey Rabbit tripped up to him. 'Good-morning, Hedgehog. Have you brought the milk?'

'Yes, and had my head snapped off by those two. They think another Weasel has you,' and he laughed grimly.

She opened the gate and ran to the house.

Hare! Squirrel! Look at my primroses, a basketful, picked with the dew on them, to make Primrose Wine and cure your cold, Hare!'

'I knew she was sympa-what-do-you-call-it,' cried Hare delightedly.

All day they made the wine. Grey Rabbit packed the heads in layers in a wooden cask, tightly, and between each layer she put an acorn-cup of honey and a squeeze of wood-sorrel juice. Squirrel picked the wood-sorrel and Hare pounded it with a stone. Squirrel filled the kettle many times from the brook, and put it on the fire. Grey Rabbit poured the boiling water over the flowers until the cask was full. Then she sealed it with melted bees-wax and buried it in the garden.

ow tired I am, pounding all those leaves,' said Hare, as they sat down to tea.

'How tired I am, filling all those kettles,' said Squirrel.

'How glad I am the wine is made,' said Grey Rabbit, as she poured out the tea and cut the bread and carrot.

'When can we have some?' asked Hare.

'In twenty-four hours,' said the Rabbit, and Hare began to count the minutes, and to sneeze very loudly.

That night Wise Owl flew over the house.

'Too-Whit, A-tishoo! Too-whoo, A-tishoo!' he cried. 'Too-Wishoo-oo-oo! Too-Whoosh-oo-oo!'

As he flew far over fields and woods there came a faint Tishoo-oo-oo floating in the wind.

'Poor Wise Owl,' murmured Grey Rabbit to her blanket, 'I must take him a bottle of Primrose Wine, too.'

The next day Squirrel, dressed in a brown overall, worked in the garden, digging the soil, raking the rough little knobs with her scarlet-handled rake, and sowing fresh dandelion and lettuce seed.

Hare sat sneezing by the fire, playing noughts and crosses against himself. He always won, so he was happy. Besides, he kept thinking of the wine, and counting the minutes.

rey Rabbit had some sewing to do. She sat in the rocking-chair making new white collars and cuffs for herself, and mending her torn apron. Then she made a red Sunday coat for Hare, and a yellow dress for Squirrel. Her needle ran in and out, and the tiny bobbins of cotton emptied themselves as she sewed, until two white, three red, and three yellow ones rolled on the brick floor.

At last she finished and put away her work. Squirrel came in, stamping her feet and crying out against the cold.

'It's bitter today, Grey Rabbit. Where's my teazle brush? It's time you got me another.'

Grey Rabbit found the brush in the wood-scuttle, where Squirrel had thrown it.

23

S he brushed and combed the Squirrel's tail until it was glossy and bright again. Then she picked up the bobbins, and strung them on a horse-hair ready to give to Hedgehog when he called with the milk.

After dinner she left Hare explaining how to win at noughts and crosses to Squirrel, who could never understand, and away she went over the brook and through the Wood with her basket.

The trees were bare, but here and there a honeysuckle waved tender green leaves as it climbed up a nut-tree. The Rabbit stopped to taste these, and put a few in her basket to mix with the salad for supper. Next she picked some stiff little purple buds from a low-hanging elm.

She looked longingly at a horse-chestnut whose sticky buds were beyond her reach.

'If only Squirrel would come in the Wood again,' said she, 'we could have such delicious meals!'

It was very quiet here; no rabbits ran among the undergrowth, no birds sang in the tree-tops, only now and then a rook flew overhead with a rough 'Caw, Caw,' or a pheasant scattered the beech-leaves which covered the ground. The Rabbit's heart thumped, she was always nervous in this Wood. Her ears were pressed back and her eyes looked all ways at once, but nothing came to alarm her. At last she ran through the gate and entered the Teazle-field.

She bit off a few heads, all dry and prickly, and then she filled her basket with curling shoots of young green bracken, which she found hidden under the dead-gold fronds, and knobby fern-buds from under a wall.

Home she ran, softly through the Wood, stepping on the soft moss and mould, and avoiding the rustling leaves.

'Robin Redbreast has been with a letter for you,' said Squirrel, emptying the basket in the larder and putting the brushes in a cupboard.

Grey Rabbit took the tightly-sealed leaf-envelope, and broke open the brown flap.

'Who is it from?' asked the curious Hare.

t's Moldy Warp's writing,'
answered Rabbit, as she turned
the letter up and down, inside
and out.

'What does it say?' asked Squirrel.

'It says "Found Knock Mole,"' said
Rabbit.

'Whatever can it mean?' they all asked.

Hare said, 'Moldy Warp has been found
knocked over.'

Squirrel said, 'Mr Knock has found Mole.'

Grey Rabbit said, 'Mole has found a
Knock, but who has lost one?'

As the evening wore on Hare got more and
more excited, until he could hardly bear to
wait for Rabbit to dig up the cask.

The seals were broken and such a delicious smell came into the room, like pine forests, and honeysuckle, and lime-trees in flower. Hare and Squirrel ran for their blue-rimmed mugs and dipped them in the cask. They came out filled to the brim with a golden thick syrup.

'Good! good!' said Hare, smacking his lips, 'I feel better already.'

'Beautiful!' sighed Squirrel in a rapture.

Grey Rabbit filled a bottle and tucked it under her arm. 'I'm going off at once with this bottle to Wise Owl,' said she. 'He sneezed all over the sky last night,' and before they could protest she had gone.

I t was a dark night, the moon had not risen, but the stars in Orion's belt shone down and lighted her path in the black Wood, as she hurried along to the tree where Wise Owl lived. She would have to be quick to catch him before he went out hunting. The Wood was full of little sounds, rustles and murmurs. What were they? Grey Rabbit did not know; she only felt very frightened, for they were not comfortable homely sounds. She looked up at the blinking stars, and the way seemed clear.

'A-tishoo! A-tishoo! Tishoo!' came echoing through the trees, and she caught sight of Owl's shining eyes, and her own little white tail hanging on the door of the big oak tree.

'Is it lonely too?' she wondered.

She waved her handkerchief as a truce, and Wise Owl nodded to her. 'A-tishoo! A-tishoo!' said he.

'Wise Owl, I've brought you some Primrose Wine for your sneeze,' said she.

He hopped down and took the bottle from her trembling paw.

'Thank you, Grey Rabbit, thank you kindly,' and opening wide his beak, he drank all the wine and then swallowed the bottle.

'That's good! Even old Owl could not make Primrose Wine. What would you like, Grey Rabbit?'

She hesitated and looked at her forlorn tail.

o, Grey Rabbit, I could not part with that, unless you bring me a bell to go Ting-a-ling-a-ling when visitors call. Then you shall have it. But here is a book of riddles.'

He gave her a little green book of Owlish jokes.

'But, Wise Owl, where shall I find a bell?' said poor Grey Rabbit, who sadly wanted her tail.

'In the A-tishoo! The world is full of bells and A-tishoos,' sneezed Wise Owl, and he raised his great wings, and flew over the Wood.

Grey Rabbit ran home again with the book in her paw, but her thoughts full of the bell.

The murmurs in the Wood became fainter as Owl flew over, and now the white moon, beloved of all rabbits, was slowly rising over the hill.

Squirrel and Hare were sitting up for her, with a mug of mulled wine on the hob, and between them, sipping from a tea-cup, sat the Mole.

'Here she comes! here she comes!' they cried, as the latch rattled and she flung open the door.

'Mole has something for you,' said Hare excitedly.

Mole brought out a large silver penny, with an eagle on one side and an emperor on the other.

'It's Roman,' he said.

'I found it deep down in the earth, and I thought it would do for Wise Owl's door-knocker.'

'Oh, you kind Moldy Warp! Do you mean instead of my tail? Alas! Wise Owl wants a bell; he will give it to me for a bell.'

'A bell? A bell? Where can we get a bell?'

'A bell rings people to Church,' said Hare.

'There is a bell in the village shop,' said Grey Rabbit.

'A bell calls the children to school,' said Squirrel.

'There are Hare-bells, Blue-bells and Canterbury-bells,' said Hare.

'I might make a bell,' said the Mole, holding the penny in his strong hands.

will bend it and bend it and twist it with my fingers till——,' and he walked musingly out of the house.

'Good-night, Good-night,' everyone called after him, but he only said, 'And bend it and twist it and bend it,' as he went slowly down the garden path with the moonlight on his silver penny.

Hare took the book of riddles to bed with him, and prepared to astonish Squirrel with a joke. But when he awoke without his A-tishoo, he felt so grateful to Grey Rabbit that he got up early, and went out into the fields to look for bells.

When Grey Rabbit had filled the little blue-rimmed mugs with milk, and put the dandelion leaves on a dish, the nuts on a plate, and the salad of buds in a bowl, she called Hare.

'Hare, Hare, come to breakfast.'

Hare came scampering in. 'I've been looking for Hare-bells,' said he, 'but the Spinks say there are no Hare-bells in March, and they called me a March Hare for looking for them.'

'I'm going to the village shop to get that bell,' announced Squirrel.

'Oh, Squirrel!' exclaimed Grey Rabbit, 'please don't. The old woman might catch you.'

'That she never will,' laughed Squirrel, but secretly she was frightened at her own daring.

fter dinner, when the old woman had her nap, Squirrel started off. She put on her best yellow dress, and her little blue shoes, and she tied her tail with a bow of blue ribbon.

'You never know who will see me,' she said, as she admired herself in the glass.

'Run for your life if anyone does see you,' said Hare warningly.

She ran with a hop and a skip down the lane, leaping over budding brambles, stopping now and then to eat a green sycamore bud. Under the brambles white violets were hiding in their bunches of leaves, and she picked a small bunch.

She entered the village, and found all quiet, except for an old farmer, jogging home behind his brown mare.

She ran swiftly across the empty market-place to the shop, but the door was shut, so she hid in a garden near.

Presently a woman came out of a cottage and pushed open the shop door. Tinkle, Tinkle, went the bell.

'It's still there,' said Squirrel, running in after her.

'A pound of candles, please, Mrs Bunting,' said the woman. 'And how's your cough?'

'It might be better, Mrs Snowball, and it

might be worse,' said Mrs Bunting, reaching for the candles.

'Well,' said Mrs Snowball, 'you should get an onion, and boil it, and then bake it, and then mix it with——'. But her sentence was never finished, for the Squirrel, crying, 'Death or Glory,' leapt at the bell, and tugged and bit and pushed.

The two women shrieked as the jangling bell banged violently backwards and forwards with a yellow animal swinging on it.

'It's a monkey, a great yellow monkey,' cried one.

'No, it's a wild cat, a great yellow wild cat, with a blue ribbon,' shouted the other, and they both ran screaming to the Blacksmith next door.

quirrel kicked her shoes off and lost her blue bow, but she forced the bell, and fell with it to the floor, knocking over three buckets, a milk-can, a mouse-trap, and a basket of eggs. Such a din and clatter came from the shop! Squirrel picked up the bell and ran out of the door, jingling-jangling through the market-place.

'There it is, there it is, Mr Blacksmith. That's the creature and it's got my bell,' cried Mrs Bunting.

The Blacksmith threw a hammer after Squirrel, which hit the bell, making it ring even more.

'My daughters will say it was another rabbit, when they come home,' said Mrs Bunting angrily.

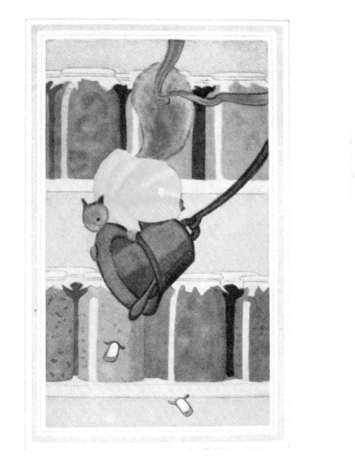

I t's my opinion it was a Squirrel, ma'am,' said the Blacksmith mildly, but when Mrs Bunting found a bunch of violets and a pair of tiny blue shoes, he scratched his head and said, 'It's mighty queer!'

Away went Squirrel, dragging the noisy bell with its coil of thick springs twisting round her tail. Such a rattle was never heard, and the dogs and cats awoke, barking and howling. She passed the old brown mare, who shied in a fright and nearly upset the farmer out of the cart. She banged and bumped along the road, up the lane, through the garden, and into the house.

Squirrel was a heroine that day.

But when Hare and Grey Rabbit dragged the bell across the Wood to Wise Owl's door, he put out his head with half-shut eyes and hooted.

'Who's waking up all the Wood? How can I catch any dinner with that hullabaloo? How can I sleep with that Jingle-jangle? Take it away!' And he banged his door, so that the little white tail shook.

They left the bell to rust in the Wood, and ages afterwards it was found by a game-keeper, who returned it to Mrs Bunting.

When the dejected Hare and Grey Rabbit got home they found Mole talking to Squirrel.

He had brought a silver bell, a little bigger than a Hare-bell, a little less than a Foxglove-bell, with a tiny clapper of a hawthorn stone, hung on a hair from a white mare's tail.

When he shook it a sweet silvery tinkle came from it, so delicate, so thin, so musical, that Squirrel and Hare looked round to see if a Jenny Wren was in the room, and Grey Rabbit looked out to see if the stars were singing.

All round the bell Moldy Warp had made a pattern of lines like a shell, and in the middle the eagle spread his wings. They hung up the bell by its twist of sheep's wool, and listened to the song of bees and flowers and rippling sunny leaves, and deep moss which it sang to them.

Grey Rabbit started off with it as soon as it was dusk. She felt no fear as she carried it tinkling through the thick Wood, for the Wood held its breath to listen.

'What is that?' asked Wise Owl, as he peered down from his branch, and moved his small ears.

'A bell for my tail,' said Grey Rabbit boldly, and she tinkled the little silver bell.

Owl climbed down.

'You shall have your tail, Grey Rabbit. Give me the bell. It is soft,' he went on; 'no one can hear it but our own people. It is beautiful, for it is like a flower. It is wise, for it lived in the beginning of the world.'

o he hung up the bell on his front door, and there it sang with every breeze. And he gave Grey Rabbit her soft white tail in exchange. He fastened it on with threads of Stitch-wort, and anointed it with the Herb of St John, so that by the time Grey Rabbit reached home again her tail was as good as ever.

But Moldy Warp took with him to his house under the green fields a bottle of Primrose Wine and the thanks of the little company.